SEOULFUL Kiss

JAX CASSIDY

Cassidy

For Chandler, my talented niece.
Not only do we share the same fashion sense,
but a love for guyliner, K-pop, & K-Dramas.

ONE

"Let's give a warm welcome to tonight's contestant!" The announcer grinned at the cheering crowd. He was a Vegas version of a variety show host, short and plump, and dressed in a loud red suit with a gold bowtie.

Rissa stumbled onto the stage when a co-worker pushed her forward. In her slightly intoxicated state, she still managed to remain composed. However her body wasn't communicating with her head and the contents of her stomach threatened to make an unwanted appearance. She never liked being the center of attention and this queasiness was exactly why she'd avoided these scenarios.

"So, who is this lovely lady?" He shoved the microphone under Rissa's nose and all she could do was blink, her eyes trying to adjust to the blinding brightness.

The spotlight held her rooted to the floor as a flush of embarrassment heated her neck and stained her cheeks. How could she be so naïve? Her lips bowed upward at her inability to see past the darkness, to the faces witnessing her moment of humiliation.

Don't let this phase you. Don't let them get to you.

She was sick to her stomach but managed to plaster on a bright smile.

AJA! Aja, Rissa! Fighting! Her conscience shouted the affirmation to raise her morale. She straightened her shoulders and lifted her chin. Rissa wasn't about to crumble in front of her workmates and a room full of strangers. She'd never succumbed before, and she wasn't about to start now.

A wave of dizziness snuck up on her and made her unbalanced on her feet. She sucked in a deep breath, making an effort to remain steady. The heat from the track lights didn't help matters either. Besides perspiration beading her forehead, she could certainly feel the aftereffects of one too many glasses of soju. Perhaps she should be grateful that the alcohol gave her the courage to tolerate the scrutiny. A sober Rissa was way too level-headed to wind up in this ridiculous predicament in the first place.

What a fool she was! She should've known this was all a setup. When her co-workers had excitedly suggested going out to celebrate her birthday before the holiday break, she should've followed her gut and declined. Instead, they'd used her. She didn't know what stung more—the fact that she believed they'd had good intentions, or discovering what her feelings were worth to them.

Five pounds of Kobe beef, as it turned out, and the soju bar tab settled for the evening.

SEOULFUL Kiss

She scowled. *It could be worse, right?* She supposed that from a positive perspective, at least she was being compared to an expensive cut of meat. She blew out a quick breath and shook off the anger simmering within.

The announcer pulled the mic back after her lengthy silence. "No need to be shy." He raised the note card eye-level and read out loud, "It says here, your name is Christmas Park. How festive! We couldn't have planned it better than this." The crowd laughed, some howled and whistled.

She cringed at the use of her given name and grabbed the microphone from him. "Rissa. My name is RISSA."

He yanked the mic back with a scowl. "Um, Miss Christmas Park, your friends mentioned that it's also your birthday tonight, which makes this contest even more eventful. Maybe this is it. Maybe this year someone will claim the grand prize!"

Rissa hissed, "What kind of contest is this?" His words unsettled her and she glared at him when he waved her question aside.

"It's true, folks. It's been exactly five years tonight and no one has come close to winning. Perhaps this singles crowd will be a bit more daring this year?" he hinted enthusiastically.

Again, the crowd exploded with claps and cheers.

She tugged on the man's arm to try to capture his attention. "Whoa. What? What do you mean singles crowd?"

Her workmates had blatantly lied to her about the contest. They'd told her it was a silly game of questions and answers, nothing more. Those jerks had pulled many pranks on her since she'd started with the company—from unscrewing the lid off the sugar container to switching the restroom signs so she'd wind up in the men's room. She'd never expected they'd be quite *this* cruel.

This time they'd gone too far and she wasn't going to let them off so easily. She couldn't wait until she got off the stage. There would be hell to pay!

"Since Christmas is considered a couples holiday, we wanted to bring some luck into one single woman's life!" The man's voice drowned out her plots for revenge. He continued all too cheerfully, "We've randomly chosen a card that was submitted from the mystery box. To be eligible, this woman must not have been asked on a date for at least a year, nor has she been kissed—"

"WHAT?" Rissa shrieked when his words registered in her cloudy head. "You're not serious? I'll have you know—"

The announcer ignored her protest and practically screamed, "Are you ready, single guys? This is your chance. Who's brave enough to come up here and end her kiss-free streak? The man who plants a big one on her within the sixty-second timeframe will share in the grand prize. Can Christmas Park be *the* one?" He cued the assistant to start the clock. "Let's begin the countdown!"

Yoo Min Ho lounged casually against the sofa, his eyes taking in the lively atmosphere and animated patrons. The turnout seemed to

SEOULFUL Kiss

have tripled at the Seoulful Kiss since the year before. This wasn't ideal for him for many reasons. For one, he'd started using a disguise so the media wouldn't follow him. He traded in his Italian suits for an edgier look including styling his hair differently and morphing into another persona altogether. He didn't want to take any chances due to his high-profile image. His friends opted to take his lead since this watering hole wasn't a place for wealthy class citizens to frequent.

This dining and soju bar was a hidden gem that catered mostly to the after-hours crowd. It was tucked away on the very outskirts of Gangnam, an affluent district known as Seoul's "Times Square", and was the most comfortable place to stop in after a late night at the office. The cozy, low-key ambiance was exactly why he liked it and continued to return, even if it was out of the way.

The interior design was unlike the sleek, modern luxury lounges he had VIP membership to. Instead, it was colorful and held an eclectic, Western appeal. Its mismatched furnishings, subtle track lighting, and concrete stained floors added to the charm. It also boasted exposed brick walls with enormous painted images of popular kiss scenes from American cinema ranging from *Casablanca*, *Gone With The Wind*, *Rebel Without A Cause*, to *It's A Wonderful Life*. The only indicator that it was a Korean establishment was the authentic table-top barbecues and wooden bar stools positioned in the back section.

Seoulful Kiss was infamous for two things: barbeque and soju.

He supposed now they could add this ridiculous contest to that list. Min lowered the drink as he watched the emcee embarrass another woman, yet again. This was a tradition that he wasn't particularly fond of. He'd only agreed to join his friends because he'd rather be drinking with them than sitting at home alone. His buddies would drag him year after year on Christmas Eve to see who the contestant would be. He knew the intention of the game wasn't meant to be mean-spirited, yet the event had morphed into a blown up holiday entertainment that the locals expected.

Usually, the women were willing participants who didn't mind the attention. In fact, their goal was to win since it was all in fun. Of course, the restaurant's management was known to choose the plainest women in the place to ensure there wouldn't be a winner. It was a win-win for them: they'd pack a full house, gain a profit, and never have to cash out since no one ever won.

This time, it was different.

The woman on the stage didn't seem to fit the usual mold. She was a natural beauty, petite in stature, fair in skin, but with a prudish charm that made her interesting. Even from a distance she'd affected him. Her pouty lips and big eyes sucked him in as soon as the spotlight hit, but what he was most intrigued about was her fiery personality.

His lips curled into a smile. Her accent was adorable and reminded him of the American-born Koreans he'd known from the days of studying abroad. Although his friends were familiar with Korean customs and culture, they were distinctly Western in their thinking and behavior. There was definitely something fresh and innocent about their views, and it made for engaging conversation. Perhaps she was as unaccustomed to the lifestyle here as he had been in the States. His chest squeezed and he had an overwhelming urge to protect her in that moment.

The emcee's voice broke through his thoughts. "Twenty seconds to go!"

Min tightened his grip on the glass. He was torn between wanting to leave and wanting to rescue the woman from bearing any more discomfort in the spotlight.

The cocktail waitress retrieved the empty soju bottles from the table. She glanced over at the stage and laughed. "Clearly she's not going to be the one to win the grand prize this year." She balanced her tray skillfully in the palm of her hand. "Look at her hairstyle and that ridiculous outfit." She shook her head. "You'd think they'd choose someone who had half a chance."

His head jerked up at her comment and he frowned at the woman in the skintight mini-dress. He had to admit she was beautiful, tall and slender as a model, but her looks were only skin deep. He'd known so many women just like her, and compared to the woman on stage, she didn't stand a chance. Frankly, the server was unmemorable no matter how hard she worked her assets off.

Not like the woman named Christmas. Although she appeared plain, she was completely unique, even quirky. Someone he'd remember if they were to meet in a crowd.

The server's rude comment had flipped a switch in his head and he decided to take action. Min downed the drink before slamming the glass on the table. He shot up from the sofa to his full six-foot height. Once he made a decision there was no going back. Hell, this Christmas Eve he was going to carve his own tradition. He was tired of responsibilities, tired of burying himself in his work simply because it was expected of him. For once, he wanted to do something for himself.

He wanted to recapture that feeling of living for himself again.

Min didn't think, he simply reacted. Screw consequences. He heard his friends calling after him as he strode toward the stage…and straight for the doe-eyed woman.

Everything faded around him as his eyes locked onto hers, lost for a moment in the deep, caramel color. His heart pounded against his chest like a jackhammer, his palms sweaty, reminding him of high school crushes and the elation compounded by nerves.

Every step brought him closer to her. If he'd thought she was pretty from a distance, she was breathtaking up close.

"Five, four, three—" the chants increased and so did his heart rate.

There was no time left. No time to back out now.

Min's arm shot out and he seized her waist, hauling her against him. She gasped when her eyes locked on his. He didn't miss her shocked expression, her heavy breathing, and when her lush lips fell open, he captured her mouth in a kiss that was meant to prove the crowd wrong. One that was meant to show that Rissa was a desirable prize, worth much more than what everyone else saw onstage.

TWO

The stranger had caught her off-guard during the last few seconds of the countdown to steal a kiss. His actions were as sudden and unexpected as lightning, and she didn't know what hit her. In fact, she couldn't see past the spotlight to make out his face, but those gorgeous dark eyes were the first and last impression she had before his mouth covered hers.

How could she prepare for something so surreal?

His lips were soft, his hold was firm, and she melted into him. Heck, she didn't care what he looked like as long as he kept kissing her like that! Her hands slid around his neck and she clung on. Nothing seemed to matter—least of all the damn contest or her conniving workmates. The only thing she wanted was more of this man's passionate kisses. He could only be a fantasy she'd conjured in her clouded, alcohol induced state. His kisses were intoxicating, stirring things within her that she'd tried to bury.

He tasted like soju and honey.

He smelled of fresh snowfall and winter's embrace.

He held her with a gentle strength that made her feel protected.

When he tightened his hold, her senses came tumbling back, her eyes jerked open. Wait a moment, this was real. He was real!

This kiss was out in the open for a room full of strangers to view. She pushed his chest to separate them but couldn't miss the claps, whistles, and catcalls echoing through the space. She cocked her head, squinted her eyes to adjust to the light. His face came into slow focus and she witnessed his lips curve into a sexy smile, his gaze never wavering.

Whoa.

She wanted to swoon, her knees threatened to buckle.

This man kissed her?

She blinked, taking in his perfect features. Straight nose, prominent jaw, full lips, and dreamy eyes that were dark as night. Why would a total stud want to kiss her? Her eyes swept over his form and she could see the stark difference between them. She was dressed sensibly and conservatively, whereas he was stylishly edgy and swathed in black from head to toe.

She couldn't be his type. There was no way.

Then why? Was this some kind of joke? Did her co-workers put him up to this? She wouldn't put it past them after what they'd already done.

Her eyes dropped to the floor as humiliation and anger coiled in the pit of her stomach, her hands curling into tight fists. She was too upset to look at the faces staring at her, laughing at her expense. She wasn't going to stand around and be ridiculed any longer. This wasn't how tonight was supposed to end and all she could think of was distancing herself from this place. She had to get away from the pitying stares before the tears fell, before she made more of a fool out of herself. Rissa turned and walked off the stage and out of the room with as much dignity as she could muster.

The winter chill blasted right through her as soon as she stepped out onto the sidewalk. She'd left the warmth behind, apparently along with all her belongings.

What was she thinking?

That was exactly the problem. She wasn't thinking, and now she was in a dilemma. She couldn't go back inside; but what was the alternative? Rissa hugged herself to seal in some heat as she tried to figure out what to do next. Hopefully she'd come up with a simple plan before she suffered the effects of hypothermia.

"Hey!" The deep voice penetrated her thoughts and made her head jerk up. "Christmas Park! I'm talking to you."

It was him.

She panicked and pivoted on her heel, turning her back to him. Maybe if she didn't look, he wouldn't know it was her. She stared out at the stream of cars on the busy street as if she hadn't heard him call her name.

SEOULFUL Kiss

Why did he follow her? Her teeth chattered as she tried her best to brave the freezing temperature. Hopefully he'd get the hint and leave her alone.

Rissa nearly jumped when she felt something heavy rest on her shoulders. She wanted to object, but she wasn't going to deny herself some warmth. She gave him a suspicious glare that didn't faze him.

Even with her protests, the stranger helped her shrug into her coat like a true gentleman. "You left without your things," he said from behind her. His solid frame shielded some of the bitter wind from hitting her. "You also left without claiming your prize."

She could hear the laughter in his voice and it pissed her off.

Why was he going to continue the pretense? She was already humiliated, didn't he know that? Rissa whipped around to confront the man. "You can drop the act. I know my co-workers put you up to this."

"What?" He gave her a quizzical look and she almost felt guilty about the animosity in her tone.

"I said you can leave me alone now. Joke's over. You've had your laughs. Isn't that enough?"

"Look, I don't do anything I don't want to. Never have. I don't know your workmates and I sure as hell don't know what you're talking about."

His serious tone made her lift her gaze to meet his. "You don't?"

"I don't." His hard stare caused a shiver to run down her spine.

Her eyes widened as she finally took a good look at the man. He was a total H-U-N-K! She unconsciously touched her lips.

They'd been pressed against those delectable, lush lips of his? *NO WAY!* He was gorgeous! In fact, she was sure he was the most handsome man she'd ever seen.

His dark, intense eyes and jet black hair captivated her. He possessed rock star good looks that belonged in a black and white magazine spread.

If she thought he was swoon-worthy already, she was dead wrong. His perfect smile melted the ice that had formed around her body since she vacated the building. This man was six feet of nuclear heat with a lean, yet muscled physique. From the V-collar of his sweater and thick scarf to the dark denims, leather motorcycle jacket, and all the way down to his biker boots, he was a real-life hero straight from the pages of a sexy romance novel.

Wake up, Rissa! Wake up! You're totally dreaming!

"Are you okay?"

She nodded robotically before licking her semi-frozen lips. "T-thank you for b-bringing out my stuff." Was that squeaky voice really how she sounded?

"Oh, right. I have your purse." He handed the handbag to her and she held onto the strap like it was a life preserver.

He looked at her bare hand and he frowned. "Do you have gloves?"

"Excuse me?" She blinked and reality came into focus.

SECULFUL Kiss

He didn't wait for her response as he dug into his jacket pocket to pull out a pair of leather gloves. "Here, put these on."

"It's alright. I'll just catch a taxi and will be home in a matter of minutes."

He took charge and seized her hand, assisting her with the gloves. "You can't do that. You can't go home."

Her eyebrows furrowed together. "Why not?"

He looked up and gave her a devilish grin and proceeded to pull off his scarf to secure it around her neck. "Aren't you going to take responsibility for me?"

"Responsibility?" She wasn't sure what he was talking about and it didn't help that she couldn't pull her eyes away from his face. She slapped away his hand and adjusted the scarf. He was being much too attentive for her taste. Besides, his touch was making her stomach flutter.

"You claimed a kiss from me. That means you're responsible for spending Christmas Eve in my company." He cleared his throat. "I don't hand out kisses easily. You should take responsibility."

Rissa took a step back so she could breathe again. "Hold on a minute." The truth was that his closeness was totally messing with her rational thoughts. "Are you nuts? We're not filming some drama. I'm not going to be responsible for anything, mister."

"You're telling me you're not going to do the right thing after I helped you win?"

"Why don't you just go back inside and claim the prize? I don't need it, and after what my co-workers pulled, they can settle the tab themselves." She pulled the purse strap over her head and it swung across her hip like a messenger bag. Rissa gave him a glare and marched off before she decided to have a change of heart.

She paused in mid-stride.

Was he laughing at her? She could hear his rich tone and she whipped around, sticking her tongue out at him like some adolescent schoolgirl. His laughter only escalated. Why did he have to be so bloody cute? She repressed a smile and continued on her way.

Truthfully, if she stayed another minute longer, she might be crazy enough to take him up on his silly request. However, the sensible Rissa would never accept something so ludicrous. She kept walking with heavy-footed steps. The alcohol was slowly working its way out of her system and she was relieved to have her senses return.

Why did she feel so conflicted? A part of her was relieved, but another part was disappointed that he didn't follow. This was one of the most unpredictable days she'd ever had and she was ready to seek solace in her tiny but cozy apartment. The further away she got from the Seoulful Kiss, the more her irritation seemed to subside.

There was a bounce in her step by the time she made it down the block. She was still too sensitive to laugh about what had happened tonight, but she could easily add this to her list of most memorable experiences.

Her footsteps slowed as her high heels bit into the back of her ankle, making the flesh raw from the friction. God, her feet hurt. It had been busy in the marketing department of the tourism office. The holidays only added to the pressure to pull in more visitors to boost the economy. With some of Korea's celebrities infiltrating the U.S. market of late, there was an explosion of vacationers pouring in which meant added campaigns to keep the momentum.

Thinking of work always left her with a pounding headache. Thank goodness she had four full days off to bum around in pajamas and stuff her face with junk food. She'd missed having time off. Seoulites were hardcore workaholics, and from that perspective, she seemed to fit right in. A six-day-a-week work schedule was grueling; but even so, there were months when she worked through her only day off.

Jeez, why was she still thinking about work? It was a holiday weekend—*and* her birthday. She needed a mental break, but her head always wandered back to the stacks of reports she needed to finish on her return.

Rissa blew out an irritated breath. She'd worry herself to death if she didn't relax. Hadn't her best friend Valentina given her grief about this often enough? The thought of drawing a warm bath before burying herself under the heated blanket and curling up with a good book started to appeal to her. A birthday was just like any other day. So what if she didn't make a big deal out of it? Tomorrow she'd spend the day relaxing, with no distractions or stressful last-minute trips to the store to stock up on supplies for elaborate holiday dinners.

She was free.

She was completely and utterly on her own, accountable to and responsible for no one.

ALONE.

The single word echoed through her thoughts and her heart sank. She missed not seeing her parents for their usual holiday tradition in sunny Florida. This was the first year they'd be apart for the holidays. As much as she wanted to object to their last-minute plans to take a Caribbean cruise with their closest friends, she didn't have the heart to spoil their fun.

Betrayal was a bitter pill to swallow, especially coming from her parents. No matter *how* eccentric they were. She sighed.

"It's time to grow up, Rissa. I can't be babied forever."

Time to make her own traditions.

She was twenty-seven for goodness sakes! As far as the Korean singles' market was concerned, she was practically an old maid.

The roar of a motorcycle engine and the squeal of the brakes made her jump. She opened her mouth to give the person a piece of her mind when the insufferable man shoved up his helmet visor. Her mouth watered at the sexy-as-hell bad boy image he painted, the fine piece of powerful machinery between his thighs.

"You might as well give up. I won't take 'no' for an answer." His boyish grin softened his serious features.

"Stalker."

"I've been called many things, but I'll take 'stalker' if it means you'll agree to spend Christmas Eve with me."

"Do I have a choice?"

He winked. "Of course. We all have choices."

"Right." She nodded unconvinced.

"The question is—do you want to take advantage of a memorable birthday event with a handsome tour guide? Or, would you prefer spending it at home alone drowning your woes in a bottle of soju and wishing you'd taken me up on my offer?"

"Get over yourself." She rolled her eyes.

Rissa crossed her arms and mulled over his words. He did have a point. The devil and angel on her shoulders weren't much use at the moment. She bit her lower lip as she weighed the pros and cons of saying 'yes'.

Hadn't she been disappointed when he hadn't followed her earlier? It wasn't as if he gave off any crazy psychopath vibes. And after all, it *was* her birthday. Maybe she shouldn't be so uptight and should actually try to enjoy what's left of the day. She'd never done anything so spontaneous before and the idea of exploring the city with this man sent youthful excitement coursing through her veins.

Clearly the devil had pushed the angel off with a pitchfork.

As if he read her thoughts, he reached for the spare helmet and held it out to her. "Hop on. You're not going to regret it. I promise."

She grabbed the object and pulled it down over her head. She took a step and then stopped. "Before I go anywhere with you, at least tell me your name."

His smile broadened and he nodded. "Fair enough. I'm Yoo Min Ho. You can call me Min. Now, does that make us friends?"

"Hardly," she laughed as she slid into position behind him, her thighs almost touching his. Thankfully, she'd worn a pantsuit today. Unusual, for her, yet for some reason she'd decided to at the last minute. Perhaps the heavens had given her a subtle clue.

She cocked her head back and gazed up at the stars. They twinkled brightly back at her as if to say she'd made the right decision.

Min revved the engine before reaching around to guide her hands to his waist. "We don't want you falling off."

The retort died on her tongue as the bike shot off and she had no choice except to hold on for dear life.

"I—I can't do it. I'm afraid of heights!" she squeaked.

"It's perfectly safe. I wouldn't steer you wrong. Besides, I'll be right there with you," Min's voice was calm as he tried to soothe her fear.

Rissa swallowed hard, trying desperately not to turn tail and run. They had arrived in Namsan Park, where the North Seoul Tower sat majestically on the mountaintop. In order to reach the famous tourist spot, she'd have to ride the cable car all the way up. The idea made her queasy just thinking about how far off the ground they'd be.

SEOULFUL Kiss

She'd seen beautiful photographs shot from the tower with its stunning view of Seoul and the surrounding areas, but seeing it up close was never something she'd planned on doing. Rissa was convinced Min was secretly out to torture her.

"You can't live in Seoul and not visit the tower. It's a rite of passage."

"Why don't we take a photo of it from here with my phone and say that we did."

He laughed and shook his head. "That's cheating. C'mon, you can close your eyes the whole way up."

She shook her head emphatically. "No can do."

Min placed his hands on her shoulders and looked deep in her eyes. "You can do. Tell you what—if you survive the trip up, I'll buy you whatever you want. I'll even let you pick the next location."

Rissa drew in a deep breath, expelling softly. "I can close my eyes?"

He nodded solemnly.

"You won't make fun of me or try to frighten me?"

He shook his head, just as solemnly.

"Swear it."

"What are we, ten?" he teased.

"Swear it or I'm not going." She gave him a determined stare.

He released his hold on her and held up his pinky. "I promise."

The pinky promise was as good as an oath, a contract between two people. How could she not trust him? Rissa hooked her pinky around his and he tucked his fingers into his palm, bending his knuckles toward hers. She mirrored his action until their knuckles met up and their thumbs connected.

This action sealed the deal.

Min led her into the Namsan cable car as she shielded her eyes and made sure her back was away from the window. He stepped in close so she was facing his chest as the rest of the tourists shuffled behind him. The car jolted and she fell forward, flat against him. They ascended slowly, higher and higher up the mountain. She squeezed her eyes shut, holding her breath as she unconsciously held on to his sweater. He wrapped his arms around her and hugged her.

She buried her face against his solid chest and a tingling sensation washed over her. Was it her imagination, or did they really fit this well?

He leaned in and whispered into her ear, "I'm here with you. Don't be afraid."

Rissa smiled against his chest. For once, she was pleased that her fear of heights had brought her closer to a man who had single-handedly brought the laughter back into her life. She inhaled his natural scent. He still smelled as wonderful as she'd remembered. Refreshing as the first, fresh layer of snow across a field of pinecones.

When they reached the top, he threaded his fingers with hers. Rissa's eyes remained focused on the ground as she followed silently behind. Somehow in a few short hours she'd grown attached, even trusted him. Something she'd never done before. This stranger had snuck through her defenses and unhinged her with a kiss, then stole her sanity with a sensuous smile.

He observed Rissa and her awed, childlike expressions brought a smile to his lips. She made her way slowly down the walkway, squeezing between—and around—the excited and boisterous crowd of tourists to read the handwritten messages on the thousands of padlocks. They were attached to the wall of fences that wrapped around the perimeter in one big loop. Padlocks in every shape and design imaginable were hooked securely to every inch of available space. Those endless batches of metal bulged out and the heaviness of the locks appeared to have warped the fencing. Although the railing seemed sturdy, the management still brought in rows of Christmas tree shaped wiring for visitors to hang their locks on. Perhaps this was meant to help alleviate some of the weighty burden on the fences.

Min smiled as he recalled her reaction at having to take another bank of elevators to the top of the tower. They'd bypassed the observatory to reach the area known as the Locks of Love. The locks represented a symbol of a couple's eternal love and the keys were thrown away to preserve that promise. Of course, when the management realized there was a potential danger of tourists being injured, they'd brought in red painted mailboxes for people to deposit their keys. Min supposed this detracted from the symbolism but he preferred this method, rather than chance getting struck by the metal keys.

Rissa straightened up when she caught sight of him. She waved him over and walked to the edge of the railing.

"I thought you were afraid of heights?"

"Somehow I feel a little secure with all these locks acting as barricades. Besides, it's dark out so the only thing I can see is building lights and twinkling stars up above."

Min raised an eyebrow at her, eying her windblown hair and her rosy cheeks, courtesy of the cold.

"What?" She gave him a big smile. "I know you're dying to say it, so go ahead and get it over with."

"Hey, I'm not going to say 'I told you so'." He crossed his arms. "But aren't you glad you came here?"

Rissa's eyes twinkled. "Uh-huh."

"Well, I figured since we're here—" He reached into his jacket pocket and pulled out a bright red, lip-shaped padlock and a sharpie. He'd purchased the items at the specialty shop while Rissa was preoccupied.

"I know this is typically something reserved for couples, but I think that since you've conquered your fear to make it this far, we should commemorate the occasion. Don't you think?"

"Lips?" Rissa crinkled her nose.

"Well, it's symbolic of our meeting, wouldn't you agree?" Min sucked in his breath when her big, brown eyes locked on his. She was a vision of beauty standing beneath the light with that innocent face beaming with happiness.

"Should we really do this?" she asked shyly.

"Uh-huh. Now, the important thing is deciding what to write." He brought the sharpie to his lips and pulled the cap off with his teeth. He lifted the lock and pressed the tip of the marker against the surface.

She shifted from one foot the other. "What do you want to write?"

He winked at her and began to write.

"What are you writing?" Rissa leaned in to look and he turned away so she couldn't see.

Min quickly scribbled the words and re-capped the sharpie. "You sure you want to read it?"

Her lips formed a silly grin. "Of course I do! Show it to me."

"My, aren't we pushy." He opened his palm and she snatched the lock.

Rissa peered at his penmanship and he pulled out his cell. She glanced up just as he snapped a picture of her. Her innocent gaze was spellbinding. Captivating.

He wanted to immortalize this moment for when the dream ended and he was back in reality.

"Hey, no fair! It shouldn't just be me. We need to be in the photo together."

He reached out and pulled her to his side. "Smile." They tipped their heads back and grinned for the camera. Rissa held the lock up between them, her head bent toward his.

"Let's get the lock on," she suggested.

He nodded, wondering why she decided not to read the inscription. He wasn't going to push the issue, though, because he didn't know what she'd think of what he'd written.

They both hung the lock on the fence and clicked it in place before sharing a laugh. He was surprised at how comfortable he was in her company. In fact, he hadn't laughed so much in a long time. There was hardly any laughter since his return to Seoul and now he realized what he'd been missing.

Friendship.

Companionship.

Real honest-to-goodness conversation with someone whose company he could enjoy, and who he knew didn't expect anything from him. He'd dated quite a few women in the past but those relationships had been tiresome. The women demanded all of his time. They took and took until he was emotionally sucked dry. That was why he'd chosen to remain single the past year. He needed to be able to breathe. He needed a clear head, so he could figure out what he really wanted.

Min shoved his hands in his pockets. "Alright, I promised I'd let you choose the next location. Where to?"

SEOULFUL Kiss

Rissa clapped her hands together, rubbing them with a lecherous grin.

He shook his head and laughed. "Should I be afraid?"

"I hope you have enough on your credit card to pay out, because it's gonna cost you."

 THREE

The delectable smells, colorful foods, and tantalizing flavors from the pojanmacha—the street food carts also known as covered wagons—made her senses go into overload. Rissa never grew tired of visiting the busy vendors in the Namdaemum market during restless evenings. She'd often wander the streets to check out the shops with their random goodies and trinkets before heading to her favorite cart run by the seventy-nine year old Mrs. Jung. The jovial grandmother was healthy and full of personality. Her warm affections reminded Rissa of having family in a city where she had none. Their relationship had quickly grown closer and she'd begun referring to Mrs. Jung as *halmeoni*, grandmother.

Tonight there was an overflow of patrons but as they approached, Rissa noticed a spot open up at the standing counter.

She grabbed Min's arm and dragged him through the crowd to claim the space before anyone could get to it.

"Halmeoni, I'm here." Rissa called out and Mrs. Jung's face lit up.

"*Halmeoni?*" Min repeated quzzically.

Mrs. Jung placed a plate of tteokbokki, stir-fried rice cakes cooked in a spicy, salty, and sweet red broth, in front of a couple before turning her full attention to them.

"I'm happy you're able to stop by. I see you've brought…" The woman's sharp-eyed gaze landed on Min. "…a friend?"

He gave her a nervous smile before he bowed his head as a sign of respect. "It's very nice to meet you. I'm Yoo Min Ho."

"At least this one has manners," she teased.

"Halmeoni!" Rissa frowned.

"Don't look so surprised, young man." Mrs. Jung gave Rissa an affectionate smile. "We don't have to be related by blood to be family. Rissa's easy to love, with her big heart and kind soul. But I'm sure I don't have to tell *you*."

"Halmeoni!" Rissa could feel her face grow hot from embarrassment. "It's not what you think."

"Oh, you don't have to protest. I can see it clearly. I may be old, but I'm not blind."

"Ahem," he cleared his throat. "Rissa tells me this is the best tteokbokki in town." Min deftly changed the subject.

"A smart young man, too!" She grabbed a plate. "How about you tell me what you think?" She reached for the ladle and scooped up a heaping portion to fill the plate before handing it to Min.

Rissa grabbed a bamboo skewer from the container and speared a piece of rice cake. She held it out for Min. "Here. Try this."

He gave her a strange look before he opened his mouth to take a bite. His eyes widened, his expression was one of pure bliss. "This *is* good!"

"Isn't her cooking amazing?" Rissa grinned.

Min nodded happily. "Yes. I stand corrected. This is the best tteokbokki I've ever tasted." He winked at Mrs. Jung. "Even better than my grandmother's cooking."

"No use trying to butter me up. It's Rissa you should be focusing on." The older woman waved the ladle at him but the grin on her face showed her delight at his words.

Rissa scowled, ready to retort, but Min quickly speared a piece of tteokbokki and popped it into her open mouth. "Eat this."

Mrs. Jung's and Min's laughter was infectious, and Rissa couldn't help joining them.

As they ate, Rissa noticed how relaxed and comfortable he was. Min got along with the grandmother and she was secretly pleased that he had the older woman's seal of approval. It was nice to meet someone so easy to talk to, and Rissa soon forgot how awful the night had begun. Now, she felt as if she'd known him for years.

She still couldn't believe someone like him was interested in spending time with her. Her eyes fell to his lips, and the memory of their kiss made her turn away.

Rissa was deep in thought when she felt his thumb graze the corner of her lips. Her eyes locked on his and he gave her a boyish grin that revealed a flash of dimples. The touch was gentle yet it left a heat that seared through her, making her stomach flutter.

"You had some sauce there." Min dropped his hand.

"Oh. Th-thanks," she stammered.

"I think I'm going to go wash my hands. Is that okay?"

Rissa nodded and pointed in the direction of the restroom. "It's up that way and around the corner."

He nodded and headed away. Only then did she let out a sigh of relief.

"He's a fine young man," Grandmother commented while she piled food on the paper plates lined up in a row. "I like that he makes you laugh. It's been a long time since I've seen you light up like that."

"It's really not what you think."

The woman handed the last of the plates to the patrons. "Whatever you say." She reached under the counter and pulled out a bag. "Here." She held it out for Rissa.

"What's this for?"

"I couldn't forget your birthday. It's not much, but I wanted to give you something."

Rissa could feel her eyes burning from emotion. "That means a lot to me." She accepted the gift and peered in the bag. "Oh my goodness, it's beautiful!"

"Don't just stare at it. Pull it out," the woman fussed.

She reached inside and took out the red scarf. Rissa grinned as she held it up, rubbing it gently across her cheek. "It's so soft and feels so luxurious! I love it!"

"I made it special for you."

Rissa rushed around the cart to give her a tight hug. "Thank you so much, halmeoni! It's the best birthday present I've ever received."

The woman feigned annoyance but she pat Rissa's arm. "Happy Birthday, dear."

"I'll cherish it forever." Rissa pulled away and immediately wrapped the handmade scarf around her neck. It instantly warmed her throat and the faint floral scent reminded her of a grandmother's warmth and love. She'd returned Min's scarf earlier so this was perfect timing, since the temperature had dropped even lower.

"Now shoo. I've got orders to fill," the elder grabbed the empty bag and sent her back around to the counter.

Today had been totally an unexpected joy and she was grateful she'd taken the chance to spend her birthday out. If she hadn't thrown caution to the wind, she'd have missed out on the adventure. The ache in her heart was no longer there.

As she waited for Min to return, she couldn't stop smiling. She wondered what their next stop would be. There were so many places she'd wanted to go and now she had someone to take her, if only for the night.

"Rissa?" a deep voice called out from nearby. "Is that you?"

She glanced up and the smile on her face vanished. "Sang Ki," she breathed. He was still handsome as ever. Tall, flower boy good looks and every bit a heartbreaker.

He walked over to her with a wide grin on his face. "It's been a while." His eyes swept over her face. "You look really good."

The thorn dug deeper in her heart. He'd been the one to break up with her, and now he was pretending as if they were long lost friends. He'd called her plain and their relationship a bore before he left her for a co-worker.

Her tone was unfriendly when she spoke, "What are you doing here?"

"I guess I was thinking about you and wanted to come to the market. This was one of your favorite places to visit. I'd hoped you'd be here but wasn't sure you'd show."

"Where's your girlfriend?"

Sang answered in an embarrassed tone, "We broke up."

"Oh." Rissa bit her lower lip. Even though it still stung as she bitterly recalled their relationship, she wondered why he'd looked for her.

"Look, Rissa. I know what you're thinking." He reached for her arm. "I really messed up. I miss you. I'm sorry I took you for granted. I really am."

33

She didn't realize Min had returned until she saw him throw Sang's hand off of her and pulled Rissa to his side. "Who's this?" Min's voice was hard as he wrapped an arm possessively around her waist. She tried to break his hold but he held onto her.

"Who the hell are you?" Sang snapped.

"I'm Rissa's boyfriend, that's who."

Sang's face dropped in disappointment. "You are?"

She cocked her head back to look at Min and her throat constricted. *Omo!* He was so handsome when he looked like that! Protective and in total control. Somehow he managed to wipe away all the bad memories she'd ever had with Sang in one fell swoop.

"Uh-huh. He...he's my boyfriend." She nodded, playing his game. She turned to give Sang a smug smile.

She eyed her ex and it hit her that he fell short on so many levels. In the four months she'd dated him, he'd never made her feel as important as Min had in less than twenty-four hours. How did she not see it before?

Min made her feel valuable. Important.

"I'm sure whatever business you have with Rissa is over."

Sang frowned. "It is now." He gave Min a strange look. "You look familiar. Do I know you?"

"I don't think so."

"Aren't you the CE—"

"No. You've got the wrong person," Min interrupted. "Now, if you'll excuse us. I'm celebrating my beautiful and exciting girlfriend's birthday."

SEOULFUL KISS

"Uh-huh." Rissa nodded her head robotically, mesmerized by Min's ability to make her feel like they were actually dating.

Sang pressed, "You're him. I'm certain of it."

"I just have one of those familiar faces," Min responded.

Sang's eyebrows knitted together. He glanced from Rissa to Min. "But how is it possible—"

Min interrupted Sang by calling out sweetly to Mrs. Jung. "Goodnight, halmeoni! We'll see you again soon."

Rissa added, "Thank you again for the present! I'll be by tomorrow."

The elderly woman grinned at them, "Happy birthday, Rissa! You kids have fun!" Her eyes moved to Sang's face and she scowled before resuming her task in a disgruntled manner.

How was it possible that Sang didn't seem to affect her anymore?

The heartache was replaced by relief. Seeing her ex again in the flesh made her wonder what she'd ever seen in him in the first place. Everything she'd once found charming no longer appealed to her. Beyond his good looks, she could finally see their vast differences. He'd never seen her as anything more than someone to turn to when he had no one else. She deserved better. She would never put herself in a position where she'd be unappreciated and considered unimportant in anyone's eyes.

Min reached for her hand and she held on tight. He squeezed gently and she smiled, delighted to see Sang's displeasure. The man needed to be knocked down a few pegs after the heartache he'd put her through. Just seeing the regret written all over her ex's face was the best revenge she could have hoped for.

She glanced over at Min and couldn't help appreciating the new tradition they'd made after all.

Rissa walked ahead of him with bright eyes and an infectious smile. How could anyone ever view her as plain? She absolutely glowed with her curiosity and childish wonderment. He watched her amble over to the crowd that formed around a local street musician. She managed to push her way to the front of the line while Min stayed behind her, shielding her from harm.

The singer strummed his guitar, belting out a heartfelt ballad about a girl he'd met by chance and the love he'd lost by not speaking up. Min glanced down at Rissa and notice a tear trickle down her face. She was a big softy. He smiled at how easy it was to read her. She was proud and prickly on the outside, but tenderhearted inside. He slipped an arm around her shoulders and leaned her close against his chest. She tilted her head up in surprise and he smiled down, quickly feigning interest in the song. His heart hammered in his chest at the unexpected way she'd grown on him, at how much he liked holding her close like this, and at how much he wanted to get to know her more.

SECULFUL Kiss

He'd been in relationships before but this woman made him feel things. What started out as something as simple as wanting her company to pass the time turned into one of the best dates he'd ever had. He didn't want the night to end because tomorrow he would have to shelve this adventure away as if it were a dream. How could they fit into each other's world? As a matter of fact, how would she react when she discovered who he really was?

Yoo Min Ho was a third generation chaebol, born into a powerful and wealthy conglomerate family. Educated since birth to be a successor, he'd become a young CEO of Yoo Construction when his father unexpectedly fell ill. He liked the thought that Rissa knew nothing about him except for his name. She'd agreed to spend time with *him*, and not because of his bank account or family status. At least then he knew whatever intentions she had were purely innocent. Unlike the women who pursued him for the sole purpose of one day becoming a chaebol's wife.

When tonight ended he wanted it to be on a good note. He'd keep the memories locked in his heart. Tonight he was simply Min, an average man on a date out, doing regular things that couples did without scrutiny or apprehension.

In truth, he didn't want to keep the secret from Rissa, but he thought it was better this way. Once tomorrow came, he would turn back to the life that was paved for him…without her. So why did it bother him so much? He couldn't afford becoming attached to this person knowing he would only hurt her. Not intentionally, of course, but if there was a chance of something more, she'd never be able to endure the scrutiny and pain caused by those on the outside.

He'd been there before. He'd seen it firsthand.

Min pushed his troubled thoughts aside to take in the scenery. Christmas Eve seemed to appeal to the masses as they celebrated along the streets and filled up the venues. This section of Hongdae surrounded Hongik University and was considered the center of Korea's youthful nightlife. Lately this area had attracted foreigners with its urban arts, indie music culture, nightclubs and entertainment. It was the go-to place for the twenties and thirties crowds to let loose.

He'd spent most of his university years frequenting this spot with friends. This place held fond memories for him, but those days were long gone. He missed his youth and the lack of responsibility. Things were much simpler back then, but time—and life—had changed him. Hardened him.

However, being here with Rissa tonight made him see another way to balance things he'd thought weren't possible. It also made him view Hongdae in a different light. Perhaps maturity made him appreciate trading the loud clubs and boisterous drinking buddies for a low-key outing with a woman who made him smile again. Laugh again.

"Wow! His voice is amazing! I can listen to him all night," Rissa practically gushed.

"Is that so?"

She turned to face him. "You don't think so?"

"He's all right." Min shrugged his shoulders.

"You're kidding me? He's fabulous!" She pursed her lips. "I bet you couldn't do better."

He gave her an incredulous look. "You had to go there, didn't you?"

Rissa crossed her arms. "I dare you."

Min leaned his face closer to hers. "You play dirty." He lowered his voice a notch, "What is your request?"

She flung open her arms and said all too loudly. "Sing for me!"

The crowd turned to observe their conversation. Min shook his head. "You're going to regret this."

She squealed, clapping her hands together. "Sing for me!" she bellowed again. "It's my birthday wish. Sing Sing! Sing!"

He blew out a deep breath. "You *would* do this to me. What happened to the prudish girl in the soju bar?"

The singer grinned upon overhearing their conversation. He slid off the stool and walked over to them. He held out his guitar to Min. "You're not going to disappoint your girlfriend on her birthday, are you?"

Rissa's face suddenly turned pale. "You can sing, can't you?"

Min shrugged. "Maybe I can." He took the offering and witnessed a flash of regret in her expression.

"Um, maybe you should've told me you couldn't sing." Her eyes widened and she squealed, "Can you even play a guitar?"

Min gave her a half smile and shook his head. She turned white as a sheet. "Now's the time to start praying," he suggested before leaving her side to take a seat on the empty stool.

The crowd clapped and whistled in approval. A woman chanted nearby, "Grant her birthday wish! Sing for the woman you love!" The audience soon followed suit with a repetitive chant, "Sing for her! Sing for your love!"

Min held the guitar firmly, placing his fingers on the chords, and sucked in the cool night air. He plucked a few chords and his eyes met hers. Rissa's hands were locked together as if in prayer. She looked as if she was expecting a disastrous solo, maybe begging for some kind of divine intervention.

His lips curved into a mischievous smile before he strummed the guitar.

FOUR

Who was this man?

Rissa had never met anyone who possessed intelligence, talent, style and good looks all rolled up into one. She stood dumbfounded as she listened to his rich voice belting out the familiar tune "Hiding My Heart" by Brandi Carlile. His pitch was perfect, his accent as American as her own native tongue. With every verse the invisible string pulled her closer and closer to this man. He handled the instrument as if it was a part of him, his powerful tone was raw and emotional. Min looked the part of an idol, a gorgeous celebrity engaging his audience as he weaved a magic spell around her.

Her eyes were drawn to his face, from the tip of his straight nose to his dark eyes, down to his lush mouth.

Was it possible to fall for someone so hard and fast?

She bit the corner of her mouth trying to snap out of the ridiculous daydream. They were merely two strangers brought together by a kiss. Yet how could she explain the common bond they shared, that she couldn't quite seem to shake?

As she listened to him sing, she couldn't help seeing a flash of a future that might possibly happen in a parallel world, but she knew it was impossible in this particular one. Just for today—for her birthday—she was going to hold onto the beautiful memory they'd made together. She was going to be Cinderella and he would be her Prince.

The song ended with a prolonged silence as the entranced crowd stared with momentary awe. Suddenly an eruption of cheers and whistles filled the air and snapped her out of the hazy fog. Min stood up abruptly and placed the guitar on the stool before he took several long strides to reach her. They were inches apart, staring without words.

Speaking with their eyes.

Kiss me!

As if in a dream, as if he'd heard her, he cupped her cheek and drew her to him. His free hand seized her waist right before his head swooped down and his lips claimed hers for the world to see…again. Their icy lips merged and warmed, heating up their souls as she gripped his shoulders and melted right into him.

If this was a dream, she would see it through to the end. She would give her heart without reservations or fear—only for today.

SEOULFUL Kiss

She held on tight to Min's hand as they walked along the street, stopping every so often to admire local artwork or souvenirs and trinkets offered at the outdoor shops. They continued down the strip where elaborate murals, everything from cute cartoony-style Hello Kitty paintings to detailed portraits and cityscapes spread across the building walls. The eclectic and the unique made up the arts district and meshed well with the indie musicians parked in different sections throughout Hongae. It was easy to get swept up in the talent pool, on any given day, yet this visit seemed like a new discovery for her with Min at her side.

Rissa couldn't help smiling as she shyly snuck glances at him. Her lips still tingled from his kiss and she couldn't repress the giddiness boiling inside. He brought back emotions of youthful crushes and the thrill of a blossoming romance.

They had walked for a good half hour before they stopped in front of a café stand. "Let's grab some coffee to get us warmed up," Min suggested. "Then I want to take you somewhere, if you're up for it."

Rissa nodded. "Sounds good."

"Just wait here. It'll be a couple of minutes."

She watched him get in line and he turned to smile at her. She waved before rocking on her heels as she waited for his return. She was thankful for the warmth of the scarf Mrs. Jung had given her. She wondered if it would finally snow.

From beside her, she heard faint whispers growing louder.

43

"Omo!" a female voice said to her friend. "Look! Look over there! I think it's him. Even dressed like that, I can tell he's the CEO of Yoo Construction." The woman pointed in Min's direction then to her cell phone. The two women beside her leaned in for a look. Another woman in the group added, "You're right, that's him. What should we do?"

Rissa hadn't intentionally listened in on their conversation but she needed some clarification. She cleared her throat to announce her presence. "Excuse me."

The pretty woman in a fashionable get-up and fur boots whipped her head up and quirked a brow, attitude written all over her face. "Yes?"

"Can you repeat what you just said to your friends?"

The leader of the lemmings placed a perfectly manicured hand on her hips. "Are you eavesdropping on our conversation?"

Rissa forced a smile but ignored the question. "I asked if you could repeat what you told your friends."

After a few seconds of the woman's glare, she waved her hand as if she didn't have time to argue. "I said he's Yoo Min Ho. The heir to Yoo Construction." Her lips curled mockingly. "What? You think you can catch someone like him?"

Inhaling deeply, Rissa couldn't stop the throbbing pain in her head or the trembling in her hands. How could this be?

Was this the truth?

Was Min really who they said he was or was it all a lie?

It couldn't be.

SEOULFUL Kiss

He was someone just like her. An outcast, someone who was among the working class in this big city.

Why would he disguise himself and spend time with the likes of her? Unless this was some perverse joke, and she was someone to screw with just for kicks.

Had she been wrong about him all this time?

Her heart sank at the thought of how ridiculous she'd been. Did their kisses mean anything to him or was he playing a part until the end?

The truth hit home. Rissa was a fool for believing that something good had finally happened to her. She had stupidly allowed herself to hope.

The catty woman gave her a once over, then laughed out loud. "I doubt he'd give someone like you a second glance. You're just so ordinary."

The other women in the group snickered.

Rissa shut out the harsh words and asked urgently, "Are you sure it's him? You're not mistaken?"

Her question was left unanswered when the mousy woman in the group let out a frustrated breath. "What should we do? It looks like he's about to leave. Let's try to stop him."

"Omo! Omo! He's headed this way," the gawky member of the group squealed, clapping a hand over her mouth with the excitement of a hardcore fan.

Min carried two cups of coffee and walked toward them. He lifted his chin and his eyes caught sight of Rissa, then he smiled.

"I knew it!" the leader grinned. "He noticed me!" She quickly struck a model pose which she tried desperately to make look natural.

The other women didn't bother hiding their delight.

He approached them and Rissa couldn't repress the weight of uncertainty settling in her heart. The unease and disappointment made it difficult for her to focus.

The women flocked around him, creating a barrier between them. She stared at Min and his smile vanished upon seeing her expression.

Rissa shook her head, her hand flew to her mouth as she tried to repress the tears and the pain caused by his deception. She pivoted around and ran, so hard and fast that she didn't hear her name being called, over and over again. She didn't see the commotion as Min rushed after her.

She thought she'd lost him when she'd ducked into a quiet alley until he snaked an arm around her midsection to break her run. Min held onto her, hugging her close to his body.

"Don't run," he whispered. "Don't run from me without hearing me out."

She shoved at his arm but he had her in a vice grip that made her even more frustrated. Why couldn't he just leave her alone?

Truthfully, Rissa was afraid of listening to what he had to say. She wasn't the type of woman who could easily be tricked, but when she was with Min, it was difficult not to fall under his spell. He was almost perfect, the kind of man any woman would dream of wanting to be in relationship with. She didn't want to delude herself. A man like him couldn't be enticed by a woman like her.

They were so different on so many levels. The possibility of him growing bored with her after a few dates seemed very real, and meant she'd be little more than a plaything. There could never be a long-term relationship, when societal expectations and pressures had so much influence on the outcome. Rissa wasn't sure an impulsive decision to be with him was the same as enduring the rollercoaster lifestyle that came with being associated with one of the wealthiest heirs in Seoul.

Rissa trembled in his arms and Min hated that she'd learned the truth before he'd had a chance to tell her. He'd originally wanted to keep their outing as a memory but that kiss had jarred him. How could he prepare for the feelings that had penetrated his own wall and make him want something more? He knew then that he couldn't walk away from an opportunity at happiness.

He'd given up so much already.

Even knowing the consequences, Min was willing to at least try, if Rissa was willing to accept everything that came with being with him. He would have to convince her that he'd only been himself around her, but the odds of her accepting that weren't looking good.

Rissa resisted, even trying to break his hold but after a few minutes she gave up and broke down. She was trying to suppress the tears but he could feel her shaking against him. He pressed his face close to her hair and kissed her head. This action seemed to break her resolve and he was relieved when she allowed him to hug her tighter.

Min didn't know how long he held onto her but he needed to take her away to somewhere comfortable, where he could finally take a gamble and see if it'd pay off.

His hand slid down her arm to take her hand. He wasn't about to take any chances as he led her out of the alley. Since he was familiar with Hongdae, it wasn't difficult for him to navigate them through the obscure sections that would help them blend in with the heavy crowds of visitors. Min wanted to shield Rissa from the group of women who had been difficult to shake. They were as persistent as any *sasaeng* fans, those fanatical and obsessed groups that would stop at nothing to catch the attention of a celebrity.

They reached his motorcycle and he was more than ready to leave the incident behind them. Rissa was hesitant about holding onto him but she didn't have a choice once they took off. The ride was tense but she eventually relaxed on the trip back into Gangnam. He hadn't planned on taking her back to his home but it was the only place he knew would give them the privacy they needed. In all the years he'd lived there, he'd never brought anyone he'd dated to his private domain. Somehow the thought made him nervous.

Was he making a wise decision?

A part of him believed it was *unmyeong*. Destiny.

How else could he explain why being with her had woken him up from his stagnant, predictable, autopilot existence?

SEOULFUL Kiss

She'd made him feel alive again.

Could he deny those feelings? She stoked his passions and brought back the laughter he'd abandoned so long ago. Rissa was someone he should hold onto at any cost, for he didn't think he'd ever experience the same opportunity again. He had to snatch it up. He had to convince her to stay by his side, to hear him out. He needed time to convince her that this wasn't impossible.

He pressed a button on the handlebar and the gate opened for him to enter. He pulled up the driveway and parked the bike. The modern construction was completely made of sturdy, sustainable material. The glass house had steel beams, treated trees and branches that were used as decorative pieces throughout the house. It was meant to portray living in harmony with nature in a minimalistic, calming environment. Min had intentionally wanted a place to meet his simple needs yet still managed to capture the attention of those from the outside world.

He had commissioned one of the best American architects to design this house specifically for him. It was a balance of harmony and energy that he needed to escape the stressful business world. His parents had been incensed when he chose to live quite a distance from their mansion, but they had given in when he threatened to return abroad, leaving them without a successor.

"Where are we?" Rissa said as soon as she was off the motorcycle.

"My house."

"Why did you take me here?"

"Why else? So you couldn't run from me," he teased.

She scowled but he didn't find any animosity on that beautiful face.

"Basically you've kidnapped me."

He laughed. "That would require me dragging you away. Have you forgotten you came of your own free will?"

She crossed her arms. "I didn't have much say in the matter."

Min's lips curled into a smile. "Well if you're afraid of me, you can walk away and I won't stop you."

Rissa gnawed on her bottom lip, dropping her arms in defeat. "Fine! You win. I know you're not going to harm me."

"Now that the truth has sunk in, how about we go inside? I'm freezing out here."

She agreed to his request but not without giving him a surly look as she breezed past him. He punched the security code into the system and the door slid open.

Min went inside and stopped when he realized she was no longer following him. Rissa stood paralyzed with her eyes wide, mouth agape.

"You don't like it?" he asked.

She shook her head. "No, that's not it. This place is absolutely stunning!"

He relaxed. "Good. I was worried you had something against my home being modeled after a natural habitat."

SEOULFUL Kiss

"You're really too much." She rolled her eyes but her expression was genuinely sincere when she spoke, "No one could ever mistake this place for anything other than amazing. It's like a big piece of artwork!"

Min was happy to see Rissa's familiar personality creeping back out. He liked it when she was herself around him, without any pretenses. She was *real*. That's what had attracted him from the beginning.

"Why don't you take the stairway up to the roof and I'll bring us some tea?" He pointed to the section against the wall. The steps were built from wood pieces that were meticulously hand carved with unique tree branch designs carved into the panels.

He watched her curious glances, the slow deliberateness in which she admired the many distinct elements within his home as she followed his instruction. Min was proud of every detail and the design choices he'd lovingly made when it came to this place. Her appreciation only confirmed his decision that she was the right person to show his sanctuary to.

Fifteen minutes later he ascended the steps with two mugs of steaming hot ginger tea in his hands. He could see her leaning against the bamboo and steel railing as she stared up at the stars. Although the rooftop was an open space, he had built in heat lamps and heated weatherproof floors to add comfort to the area during the winter. Strategically placed trees were used as decorative focal points that flowed with the theme of his home.

There was a balance of perfectly landscaped herb and flower gardens planted in a square around the width of the tree trunk. He'd managed to convey the welcoming yet tranquil feel so that he and guests could hang out and admire the view at ease. His favorite spot was a swing bench for him to sit and enjoy the view of the beautifully lit cityscape. The pièce de résistance was the delicate lighting: tea lights hung from the many tree branches, and wrap-around lighted ropes dressed the trees and gave the entire rooftop a romantic, magical feel.

Min cleared his throat so not to startle her as he approached. Rissa turned her head and gave him a shy smile. He paused, his breath hitched in his throat at the wonderful sight. The lights cast a glow around her like an ethereal spotlight. She reminded him of a faery or some mythical siren. Her dark hair spilled across her shoulders, her cheeks a rosy shade, her mouth so lush that he was almost afraid to blink. Perhaps she would vanish like a dream; but even as he thought it, he knew all too well that she was real. How could he erase the memory of what she'd tasted like? Her kisses were like sweet nectar, her lips as soft as silk. The combination was intoxicating, addictive. No wonder he couldn't bear to let her go.

He held the mug out to her. "What do you think?"

She twisted around, leaning her back against the sturdy rail. "There are no words."

Min laughed. "I'm sure after you've had some tea, plenty of words will come to mind."

Rissa smiled brighter then. She straightened up and her expression became serious. "I really wanted to be mad at you. I had so many reasons not to hear you out but..." Her eyes dropped to the mug and she let the sentence fade when she took a sip.

"But you're going to hear me out?" He gave her a hopeful look.

Rissa gave a quick nod. "It doesn't change anything but I think it's only fair considering you did celebrate my birthday with me."

He was grateful she was speaking to him, so he knew he had only one shot to make things right. He wasn't going to lie to her. Whether she accepted what he was going to say or not, he would respect her decision. Min walked to the swing bench and sat down.

"Why didn't you tell me who you really are?"

Min drank the tea and lowered the mug. "Truthfully? I liked the fact that you didn't recognize me. Anonymity is something I don't have the luxury of having." He held her gaze. "The only time I can get a semblance of privacy is if I become someone else altogether. It's worked for a little while but I knew it wouldn't last."

Rissa took a seat beside him and settled back against the bench. "After seeing those women's reactions, I can see where you're coming from. Why you'd want to go unrecognized."

"I know it's a life I can't pretend doesn't exist, but sometimes I get tired. Sometimes I need to be able to breathe." He turned to her. "Today was the first time I felt like myself. I'd forgotten what it was like to just live without worrying about reporters and fans."

She bit her lower lip. "You're practically a celebrity. But what I don't understand is why—"

"Why I kissed you? Why I chose to spend time with you? That's what you really want to know."

"Yes. I'm not someone...I'm not a person that someone like you would take a second glance at."

Min reached for her mug and placed both of their drinks on the side table that was made from a tree stump.

"Why not someone like you? I'm nothing special. If not for my family's name and wealth, I would be just like you. I'd be a regular working class citizen without any hassles or pressures that comes with the title. I'd have freedom to come and go as I please, without the need of bodyguards and disguises." He expelled a deep breath. "I'm not saying that I don't appreciate what I have. I do. I simply needed someone real to connect with. I don't like not trusting anyone and I want to be able to be myself without any pretenses."

"I'm sorry I misjudged you." Her gaze was tender and he was compelled to reach out for her but he stopped himself.

"I can't say I don't blame you. It's not a habit for me to kiss just anyone. These lips are sacred lips," he boasted in an attempt to see her smile again. Instead, he received a laugh.

"Well, are you saying my lips aren't sacred? I'll have you know these lips are worth the very expensive grand prize in a kissing contest *and* I plan on collecting on it."

SEOULFUL Kiss

"Touché!" He nodded in agreement. "However, I think I deserve to share in on it. Without a partner in crime, there was no chance of winning," he teased.

She slapped her forehead. "Right! How could I forget the accomplice? I'll be happy to share the winnings. Say a third."

He scowled. "So cheap! It should be fifty-fifty."

Their light-hearted conversation broke whatever tension had existed between them. His eyes took in her lovely face and the happiness in his heart detonated, sparking like firecrackers. Being in her company now was as natural and calming as this house he'd built. Her down-to-earth and grounded personality stripped off, layer by layer, the heaviness around his soul.

Rissa crossed her arms and admired the view in front of her. Min used the opportunity to push the swing with the weight of his legs. They rocked on the bench for a few minutes in silence.

In the distance the bright lights glittered across the horizon and he drank in the beauty that was on display. They shared a peaceful moment, lost in their own thoughts.

"It's been lonely for you, hasn't it?" she asked in a quiet voice.

Min hesitated before answering, but reminded himself that he'd told her he'd be honest. "Yes. Sometimes it's so lonely the only way to ease the feeling is by burying myself in my work."

She twisted around to face him. Her eyes locked on his. "Let's say, just for today, that I'm your special friend. Someone you can be yourself with. How about it?" Her smile brightened hopefully. "At least until the sun comes up."

FIVE

Why did she feel so nervous?

Rissa's heart pounded swift and hard, blood rushing through her veins as she waited for his response. They'd spent all this time together but right now they were on equal footing. The trust and truth was laid out in the open and she believed that from this point forward, they were just two people with nothing to hide.

She frowned when he continued to stare at her without saying a word. "You don't want to?"

The corner of his lips curved upwards. "No."

"No?"

"I meant it as a 'no', I do want. I want very much." His devilish smile reached his eyes, making his handsome features become even more prominent.

She sucked the cold air between her teeth but recovered quickly. Rissa slapped his shoulder to throw him off. "If it wasn't my birthday

I'd totally make you regret waiting so long to respond to my sincere proposal."

"That was sincere?"

She swatted at his arm again and he flinched, his rich laughter reverberated through the space.

"Truce. I call truce!" he exclaimed.

"I graciously accept your surrender." She gave him a smug smile.

He rubbed his arm but his teasing stopped. Min straightened up and dug into his pocket. "Happy Birthday, Christmas Park." He slowly pulled out the object and opened his palm to her.

Rissa couldn't seem to speak. She was choked up over the precious object. "It's beautiful," she breathed.

"I thought it would look pretty in your hair."

Her hand shook as she reached for the hairpin embedded with crystals that formed the shape of pink-toned lips. Min immediately closed his fingers over hers, holding her hand captive between his palms.

She raised her head and his expression, his eyes, melted the ice completely around her heart.

"I know we've just met, but I want you to know that this isn't the end. I want this to be the beginning of our story. I want us to be real friends." He paused. "I want this to be a promise that there will never be lies or barriers between us. Can you believe me? Can you trust me?"

Did she really hear those words? Did Min want to spend time with her, not because of a kissing contest or a birthday wish, but because he wanted to get to know her better?

"It won't work. You know there's going to be resistance and consequences. Do you really want all that?"

"I've never been more certain of anything in my life. Just as long as you're strong beside me, it will work. You'll see." His eyes pleaded with her and she glanced away.

A part of her was petrified, the other part was eager to see if it was really possible. Deep down inside, Rissa knew the answer. She was afraid it would be a hardship for him. Even if she could endure the road ahead, she wondered if she could stand by and watch the public ridicule him for his decisions. Could she dare consider this possibility?

"Don't think too hard." Min took the hairpin and clipped the object on her hair. "You have until the stroke of midnight to give me your answer. Whatever it is, I will agree to your wishes."

"There." He leaned back to admire the hairpin. "It suits you."

She ran her fingers across the jewels that formed the shape and smiled. "Thank you for the birthday gift."

"You're welcome."

Rissa repositioned herself against the swing bench. "When did you find time to get it for me?"

He followed her lead and sat back comfortably. "It wasn't difficult. You were so busy mooning over all the trinkets that I was able to purchase it when you were preoccupied."

"You're a sly one," she laughed.

BOOM! BOOM!

Her head jerked up in the direction of the noise. "My word! It's firecrackers going off."

Min reached for the wool throw blanket draped across the bench and covered their legs. "It's a Christmas Eve tradition. For the grand finale."

"Grand finale?"

"The neighbors have a habit of putting on a show to celebrate. It's their anniversary at the stroke of midnight."

She gave him an incredulous look. "Are you serious?"

"The first year I moved in they dropped by and invited me to see the fireworks. There should be a huge dinner party and then the show at precisely midnight."

"That's so romantic!" Her excitement faded and she eyed him skeptically. "You're not making this up, are you?"

He shook his head. "I wouldn't dare." He crossed his heart like a good boy scout. "Now let's watch the show." Min took the opportunity to throw an arm around her shoulders and pull her next to him.

"Hey—"

"Don't protest, just watch." His tender gaze halted her protests and she leaned her head against his shoulder as they watched in silence.

Min slid his hand over hers and his touch warmed her, straight to her heart. He was making it difficult for her to refuse his proposal. If these sensations—this attraction—continued to surge between them, she couldn't walk away without at least giving it a chance.

Rissa tipped her head back to look at him and her pulse raced, her stomach did somersaults. Could she really give up before they even started? She didn't want to regret.

Unmyeong.

Destiny.

Whatever force had brought them together wasn't something she could walk away from. Did she want to walk away? Every action was painted with symbolism, a hint…from their first kiss to what led them to this moment. Was she bold enough to deny unmyeong? She felt this desire to defy the odds, defy social status and anything else to avoid looking back one day regretting that she'd been too cowardly to take a risk.

This man who had everything was willing to wager it all to have her by his side. She couldn't let him down. She wanted to help him keep laughing, to live life freely in his heart. Just as he had done for her today. Rissa touched his cheek and he smiled down, his face leaning toward her for a kiss when her cell phone jingled a familiar tune.

She pulled away, laughing nervously before pulling the phone out of her coat pocket.

"Hello mother," she said. The sound of the familiar voice brought a warmth to her soul. She listened to her mother's ramblings and then her father took over for a brief moment to wish her a happy birthday.

Rissa covered the mouthpiece and mouthed, "Sorry."

Min's response was to hug her tighter against him.

"I'm glad to hear the cruise is going well. Your new tradition suits you both." She waited for her mother to continue and then her lips curled into a wide smile.

"I can't complain. In fact, I think this new tradition has worked out just fine." Rissa looked up at Min and she winked. "Okay, well I'll talk to you in a few days. She held up the phone and made a kissing noise. "I love you both! Goodnight."

"You have a good relationship with your parents?" Min asked.

"The best kind. No matter what decisions I make, I know they will always be on my side," she said softly.

Rissa touched her face when something brushed against her skin, settling on the surface. She touched her cheek. "What's this?" She raised her face to the night sky and the light flurries rained on her. "Snow! It's really snow!"

Min held out his hand, palm up as he caught some of the white specks. "This is definitely what you call an unexpected ending to our day."

A thought crossed her mind and she reached for his hand. "Give me your cell."

"What?"

"Give me your cell phone. It's past midnight. I'll give you a response to your question." She jutted out her jaw stubbornly.

He shook his head and complied. "Here. But don't keep me waiting."

Rissa snatched the phone and scrolled through the photos they'd taken throughout the night. Her hands stopped at the image of the lock and she zoomed in. Her eyes grew wet and she blinked away the tears. She re-read Min's neat handwriting.

A kiss brought us together.
Trust conquered our fears.
Min + Rissa

She quickly twisted around so her back was to him. "Don't peek," she warned over her shoulder. She snapped a photo and turned back to face him. "Here." She held the phone out to him.

Min took the object and turned on the phone and his worried expression transformed into a happy one. He broke out into a laugh at the photo of her with a goofy smile on her face and her fingers forming the sign 'OK'.

"That's your answer?" He raised a brow at the image.

"OK," she said and repeated the gesture. "I thought you'd be smart enough to decipher my image."

"Is that so? I'll have you know I'm no dummy. I happened to kiss the prettiest girl in town to win the grand prize in a kissing contest."

Her eyes narrowed. "Is that so?"

He flashed her a brilliant smile. "Uh-huh."

"What you're saying is that you're after me for a few pounds of beef and some soju?"

Min took her by surprise and pulled her to him. His lips inching closer and closer. "Nope. It's something even better."

"And w-what was it?" she stuttered breathlessly.

"You," he breathed.

"Me?"

"Yes. And I'll get to celebrate Christmas year round."

Rissa captured his cheeks and pulled his face even closer, their lips almost touching.

"Just shut up and kiss me!"

His eyes twinkled and he finally pressed his lips against hers, kissing her with a tenderness that she hadn't anticipated.

Rissa's heart threatened to explode from elation overload.

His mouth, his tongue did things to her that made her toes curl. She reciprocated the actions and melted into him. He fisted his hands at her waist and she didn't hold back. She returned his kisses with a promise of many more tomorrows that lay ahead in their future.

EXTRAS

MEET THE AUTHOR

Jax Cassidy followed her dreams to Paris, then Hollywood to pursue a film career but managed to fall in love with penning sexy romances and happy endings. She writes contemporary, paranormal, and historical romances and is Co-Founder of Romance Divas, and award winning writer's website and discussion forum. Jax is also known as one-half of the retired writing team of Cassidy Kent. She is represented by Roberta Brown of the Brown Literary Agency.

To learn more about Jax, visit her online:

www.jaxcassidy.com
www.facebook.com/jaxcassidyauthor
www.twitter.com/jaxcassidy

If you enjoyed SEOULFUL KISS,

look for

Shibuya Moment

By JAX CASSIDY

Yoyogi-Uehara district, Tokyo
Shibuya Train Station

I stood in front of Shibuya Station, frozen amid the crowd of fashionably dressed Japanese men and women as they passed by at a leisurely, yet hasty pace. As I blocked their path on the sidewalk, some eyed me with concealed annoyance, others with blatant curiosity. In her haste to avoid me, a young woman dressed in colorful Harajuku style bumped my shoulder, jarring me back to the present. I took a deep breath and forced my legs to move.

My eyes darted from one flashing neon sign to the next until I noticed the life-size, bronze statue of Hachiko, the Akita dog, and my mind took off again. My father had often told me the story as a child while he tucked me into bed at night. The tale always touched me and I knew it by heart, yet I never grew tired of listening to his soothing tone right before I drifted off to sleep. My heart squeezed and I forced back the tears. The pain still raw from the wound of loss.

I related to the tale on a spiritual level and seeing this statue only reminded me of my father's unconditional love. My bond ran as deep and as strong as the dog for his owner. Hachiko had waited in front of the train station every day without fail, knowing that he was more than just a companion, but a family member. Knowing without a doubt that he was truly loved. One day, when the Professor did not show up because he had died suddenly at work, Hachiko loyally waited for his owner's return. He waited every single day until he died at the very spot where he had last seen his owner. That kind of love was transcendent. Profound.

I shivered. *I could feel my father's spirit with me now.*

As if he wanted to confirm his presence, a burst of wind caressed my face, tossing the ends of my long hair into tangled loops. I adjusted my knitted newsboy cap to cover my ears and shoved my hands into the pockets of my double-breasted pea coat. My oversized bohemian bag weighed down my shoulder but I didn't care. The entire contents of my life were held within it. Another gust of wind whipped by and I faced the assault head on as I trudged down the sidewalk.

I was told winters in Japan were normally short and pleasant, often accompanied by a light snowfall. I wondered if I'd catch a glimpse of the powdered miracle during my stay. The last time I'd seen snow was years ago…long before my father had been diagnosed. The memories weren't as painful knowing he was guiding me through this mourning period. Traveling with me as I absorbed the city, discovering why he loved Tokyo so much.

Why had I waited until now to visit?

A part of me had always felt alone. Disconnected. Not completely sure where I belonged being a perfect mix of Japanese and American. Not fully sure which side to embrace or compromise without appearing as if I'd turned my back on one or the other. I learned a long time ago to stay in the background, limiting my words, building a wall around me while I immersed myself in my photography. The only way I could express my feelings without having to speak the words out loud.

Growing up, my father raised me to understand my Asian culture in hopes that I would someday find an eternal link to my heritage. As for my mother, she taught me how to dream and set my wings free so I could soar. She was the reason I was here now, honoring my father's wishes. Allowing me to grasp the answers for myself, through my own eyes, at my own speed but I loved her even more for that gentle push.

I tucked the red scarf closer around my neck to seal in the warmth. I'd overheard some of the regular hotel guests complaining that the icy chill was both unexpected and unusual. I didn't really mind the weather. It was a nice change from the perpetual sunshine and sweltering heat of Florida. My thoughts easily distracted me during my lengthy walk and I soon found myself staring in awe at the rows and rows of local vendors set up in Yoyogi Park. Apparently there was some kind of winter arts festival in full swing.

I dug through my threadbare bag, my faithful traveling companion, and pulled out my trusted Nikon. My photographer's instinct kicked in as I surveyed the scene, my gaze locked on the purely elegant booths made of slick bamboo, wood, steel, and elaborate fabrics. Anyone could see the Japanese put a lot of effort and care in everything they created. The artistry and love evident in how they displayed their work, revealing the pride ingrained within their culture. In that moment, my heart swelled upon seeing the beauty I witnessed firsthand.

Lifting my camera, I pointed the lens and viewed the brightly designed festival banner from a wide angle. I did a few establishing shots before seeking out the vendors as I snapped images of them hard at work. I watched the traffic of patrons along the path, some browsing the goods. I'd always loved candid portraits and it wasn't difficult to find the unknowing subjects falling prey to my photographer's eye. All it took was a single second for me capture the perfect shot.

Photography was my outlet, my freedom. I enjoyed viewing the world second-hand; hiding behind the camera lens so there would be less focus on me. I kept others at a distance to limit conversations and inquiries about my dual race, deflecting interest from those prying into my private life. Although I was proud of my mixed heritage, too much attention always left me uncomfortable.

Joyful shrieks rang out and I followed the direction of the charming sounds. Pleasure filled the children's cherub faces as they laughed, racing off with their toys. I chased their movements until I stumbled upon an elderly couple. I couldn't resist immortalizing the image as I stole a tender moment of the silver-haired man clipping a flower barrette in his wife's hair. I turned away, swallowing the lump lodged in my throat as I latched onto a group of teenagers dressed from head to toe in punk fashion. Skinny jeans, engineer boots, studs and chains, layered graphic tops with slashes and safety pins acting as accessories. They hung around a park bench playfully bantering with one another. More stylish than intimidating.

I bit back a smile upon noticing the odd, yet perfect harmony that linked the eclectic mix of characters to a common purpose: indulging in their love for art. For the first time in months, the heaviness in my heart lifted a fraction. My face hurt from smiling so much as I continued down the aisle, occasionally stopping to snap a few shots.

Red, brown, blue, yellow, orange. The explosion of colors filled the screen as my eyes opened to the magic of the moment. The rush flooding my body and lingered as I zoomed in on the little details. Delicate porcelain figurines, wood carvings of gods and mythical creatures, detailed paintings brushed in calligraphy to abstract watercolors splashed across enormous canvases. Every style covered in one form or another with individual artistic expression. There was something for everyone.

My legs carried me through the storm of pedestrians until I came to a screeching halt. I'd hit a wall in the form of adorable senior citizens blocking me from moving forward. From the looks of the group, it would be quite a while before I'd escape the traffic jam. I twisted my body in search of an exit route while using my camera as a telescope. I paused, focusing my lens when a unique texture came into view. The object became clearer, more defined with every adjustment. I lowered my camera, my curiosity piqued, and stepped in closer for a better look at the exquisite ceramic items on display.

My heart raced at the artist's technique, a method that resembled cracking glass spreading across the surface into eloquent branches. As if they were on the brink of being shattered but held together by an invisible force. Each piece told a nostalgic tale through the color variations that formed the delicate design, completely stealing my breath away.

I picked up the teacup with a trembling hand and eyed the soothing tones of turquoise and chocolate. It reminded me of a rainstorm of despair with flurries of hope to soothe the darkness. There was something special about this piece, an oddity among matching sets of pottery.

I had to have it.

I brought the teacup to the cashier and delighted in knowing this would be a great reminder of my first visit to Tokyo. As if the man had x-ray vision, he lowered the manga he was reading to greet me with a dazzling smile. Not what I'd expected at all. Amid the ocean of dark haired, dark eyed citizens, his blond hair and bright blue eyes was the splash of color that stuck out in the black and white photograph in my head.

"Konnichiwa," his rich voice filled the silence between us. He slid off the stool and dropped the comic book on the seat before taking the teacup from me. "Is this the only purchase you'd like to make?" His perfect Japanese penetrated my cloudy brain.

Oh my! Handsome and fluent in the language. *A language I should have already mastered by default.* Embarrassment stained my cheeks since Japanese wasn't my native tongue. At least I could muddle my way through a conversation if necessary.

His eyes sparkled with humor, waiting for my response. I blinked a few times and recovered. "Um. Hi." I swallowed. "Yeah, this is it. Thanks."

"You're American," he stated in an odd accent I couldn't put my finger on.

I couldn't help staring at his mouth, a very enticing one at that. My eyes slid over his casual attire. Black pullover sweater with a sliver of white from his t-shirt peeking out over dark faded jeans. He had a swimmer's physique with strong muscular shoulders, tapering down to a trim waist, with a broad chest, and flat abs on a six foot frame. Yeah, he definitely wore his clothes well.

Hottie caught me practically drooling and his lips formed a secretive smile. "Student?" he asked nonchalantly then eyed the camera dangling from the strap around my neck. "Working?"

"Vacationing, actually. It's my first trip to Tokyo," I responded nervously.

His sultry gaze made me feel a bit shy. I grasped at any reason to break eye contact and searched inside my bag for the wallet.

He didn't ring up the item but wrapped the teacup in decorative tissue paper with a cherry blossom pattern. He pulled out a small shopping bag made from recycled paper with ribbon handles. After placing it gingerly inside, he held out the bag for me. "Domo arigato."

"How much do I owe you?" I asked, my eyes finally locking on his brilliant blues.

His boyish grin softened his features and made him look years younger. "It's on the house. My gift to you as a 'Welcome to Tokyo!'"

I shook my head. "Oh, no. *No*. I can't accept this gift. It's too valuable and the artist still needs to make a living."

"I'll make sure he's taken care of." He nudged the bag at me again. "Please accept the gift. It's customary you accept."

I bit my lower lip and finally took his offering. "That's very generous of you."

He probably wasn't aware that his dimpled smile added to the charm. "How long will you be in Tokyo?"

I had a feeling he wanted to prolong our conversation, which I was willing to participate for a little while. "Another week, maybe two, that's if I'm not called away on assignment."

"What exactly do you do?"

"I'm a freelance photographer for several news magazines, but I primarily work with *Life and World*."

He whistled. "Very Impressive. Now it makes sense why you're touting such a high end camera."

"Do you know much about cameras?"

"A little bit. It's more of a hobby. I like to take snapshots of the pottery."

"Makes perfect sense." It was a nice surprise to know we had something in common.

He ran a hand through his tousled hair, making the spikes stand up in perfect form. "You must be pretty good. Maybe I've seen some of your work before."

I gave him a secretive smile. "Maybe."

"So where are you headed next? I could give you some recommendations on interesting places to visit if you'd like."

"Thanks for the offer, but I have my itinerary planned out."

"That's very efficient." His bright blue eyes sparkled. "Well, I hope you'll have a pleasant vacation," he said huskily.

"I already have." A warm smile spread across my lips. I turned to walk away when his words stopped me. "Be careful, though."

I turned back to him. "Careful, why?"

He gave me a deadpan look. "Tokyo is an addiction. It'll spread through your veins like fire until it consumes you and you'll crave to return. Again and again."

My face relaxed and he winked when I caught on. "I'll keep your warning in mind. Have a good day—"

"Max," he filled in.

"Have a good day, Max." I bit back a smile at his obvious flirtation.

"Before you go, at least tell me your name since we're practically friends."

"How rude of me," I feigned alarm. "I'm Seren."

"Seren," he repeated. "That's an interesting name."

"Maybe someday I'll tell you all about it." I whirled around and left him staring at my back.

"Will I ever see you again?" he called out from behind me.

"Maybe," I threw over my shoulder. Walking further away, not daring to look back. Not daring to take a chance for fear that it wouldn't be wise to act on my desires. I let out a weary sigh knowing the mystery was always more enticing than the reality.

A light breeze caressed my cheek and I shuddered.

Only destiny will tell, my conscience whispered in response to the doubt rolling in my head.